The Little Mouse Who Slept.

By

John C Burt.

This is the
story of :
' The Little
Mouse Who ..

Slept?' There once was a Mouse who did the unthinkable and slept !!!

Let me now introduce you all to the Little, little, Mouse in question? Here we have 'Ella?'

Or if we are going to be all formal about it her name it is: 'Eleanor ?'...

'Ella' was the Mouse who just wanted and wanted so much to go to sleep!!!

You may not believe it but even the little Mouse 'Ella'; had too check out for very ...

9

pests and dare I say Monster's who lurked, as you would know in the darkness?

The problem that 'Eleanor' had was that as she .... checked for the very, very,

13

real pests and the Monster's who lurked, lurked, in the Darkness of the Night was..

that doing this very thing would wake her up; wake her up .. awaken her !!!

As you would remember all the time in this book : 'Ella' was just a little Mouse who ...

just wanted to
be a Mouse
who slept the
whole of the
Night - time
through ?

As you can also probably all see, 'Ella'; the little , little, little Mouse ..

carried

everywhere

with her, the

blanket she

used as a bed.

This blanket was not only her bed but also it acted as security for

'Eleanor;' the tiny, tiny, little as little Mouse. The Mouse who just wanted to

be a Mouse
who was one
who was
sleeping or at
least .....
pretending too.

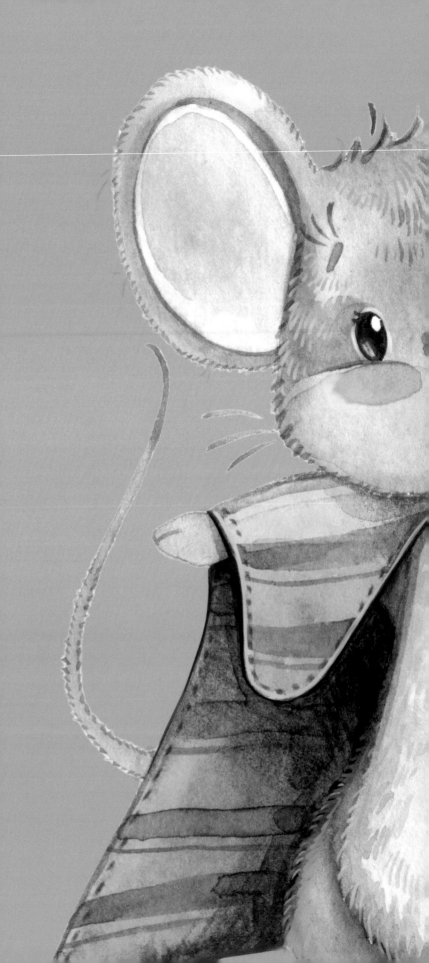

Yet, in the case of 'Eleanor' the tiny, little ... Mouse sleep..

27

sleep, blissful sleep, always, even now, seemed to be so far away from her !!!

'Ella' the tiny, little Mouse found herself, continually walking the very corridors

of the very
house she
lived in , with
her only ....
company her..

little shining lantern ... She was checking for the very pests and the Monsters who

kept her from
blissful sleep?
The sleep of
the ages is
what ' Ella '
wanted to have

33

and know she had once in her lifetime!!! Will 'Eleanor'; ever get that sleep?

Would you know it but now at this point in this very book; 'Eleanor' is asleep!!!

CPSIA information can be obtained
at www.ICGtesting.com
Printed in the USA
BVRC090843200921
617100BV00006B/52